A Beginning-to-Read Book

Astro the Alien Learns about Public Holidays

by A. M. Krekelberg

Illustrated by Carlos Aón

NORWOOD HOUSE PRESS

DEAR CAREGIVER,

Books in the Beginning-to-Read collection are carefully written to develop the skills of early readers. The *Astro the Alien* series is a step up from the introductory *Dear Dragon* series. It provides early readers the opportunity to learn about the world through the narrative while building on their previous reading skills. The text in these books is comprised of common sight words and content words to expand your child's vocabulary. Increasing readers' sight word recognition promotes their reading fluency. The vivid pictures are an opportunity for readers to interact with the text and increase their understanding.

Begin by reading the story as your child follows along. Then let your child read familiar words. As your child practices with the text, you will notice improved accuracy, rate, and expression until he or she is able to read the story independently. Praising your child's efforts will build his or her confidence as an independent reader. Discussing the pictures will help your child make connections between the story and his or her own life. Reinforce literacy using the activities at the back of the book to support your child's reading comprehension, reading fluency, and oral language skills.

Above all, encourage your child to have fun with the reading experience!

Marla Conn, MS, Ed., Literacy Consultant

Norwood House Press

For more information about Norwood House Press please visit our website at www.norwoodhousepress.com or call 866-565-2900.

© 2023 Norwood House Press. Beginning-to-Read™ is a trademark of Norwood House Press.

Library of Congress Cataloging-in-Publication Data

Names: Krekelberg, Alyssa, author. | Aón, Carlos, illustrator.
Title: Astro the alien learns about public holidays / by A. M. Krekelberg ; illustrated by Carlos Aón.
Description: Chicago : Norwood House Press, [2023] | Series: Beginning-to-Read | Audience: Grades K-1
Identifiers: LCCN 2022000754 (print) | LCCN 2022000755 (ebook) | ISBN 9781684507627 (Hardcover) | ISBN 9781684047871 (Paperback) | ISBN 9781684047932 (eBook)
Subjects: LCSH: Holidays--Juvenile literature.
Classification: LCC GT3933 .K74 2023 (print) | LCC GT3933 (ebook) | DDC 394.26--dc23/eng/20220204
LC record available at https://lccn.loc.gov/2022000754
LC ebook record available at https://lccn.loc.gov/2022000755

Hardcover ISBN: 978-1-68450-762-7   Paperback ISBN: 978-1-68404-787-1
353N—082022
Manufactured in the United States of America in North Mankato, Minnesota.

"Where are you going?" asked Eva.

"School," said Astro.

"We do not have school today. It is Presidents' Day," said Ben.

"What is that?" asked Astro.

"It is a holiday. It celebrates US presidents," said Eva.

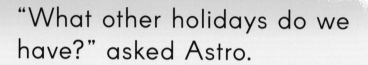

"What other holidays do we have?" asked Astro.

"There are a lot," said Eva. "They are all on different days."

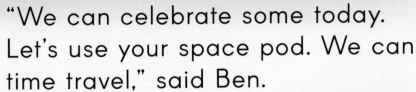

"We can celebrate some today. Let's use your space pod. We can time travel," said Ben.

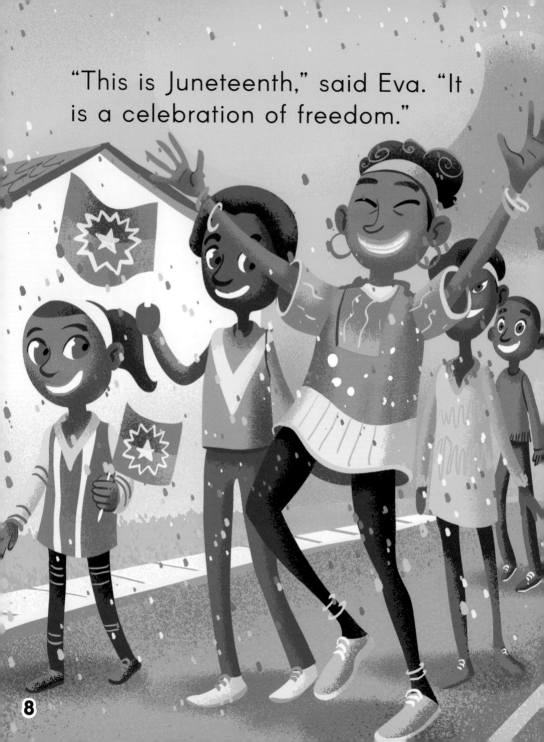

"This is Juneteenth," said Eva. "It is a celebration of freedom."

"It happens on June 19," said Ben.

"The United States used to have slavery," said Ben.

"It ended in 1865," said Eva.

"Enslaved people in Texas were told about it on June 19. They celebrated their freedom," said Ben.

"Today, many people celebrate Juneteenth," said Eva. "It is a very special day."

"People make speeches," said Ben.

"There is also good food," said Eva.

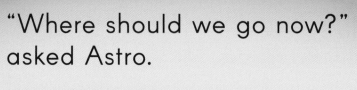

"Where should we go now?"
asked Astro.

"I know!" said Ben.

"I like the Fourth of July," said Ben.

"This is when we celebrate our country's beginnings," said Eva.

16

"And watch fireworks!" said Astro.

"This is Indigenous Peoples' Day," said Ben.

"It celebrates Native Americans. It is on the second Monday in October," said Eva.

"Some people celebrate by dancing," said Ben.

"Other people sing," said Eva.

"We can learn from traditional artists," said Eva.

"We can see beautiful things people have made," said Ben.

"This is Veterans Day. It is on November 11," said Eva.

"This holiday celebrates veterans. They worked in the military," said Ben.

"They protected our country. Some even fought in wars," said Eva.

"There is a parade!" said Astro.

"I hear music," said Ben.

"I think it is time to go home," said Eva.

"There are a lot of important holidays. It is good to know more about them!" said Astro.

29

Comprehension Strategy

To check your child's understanding of the book, recreate the following diagram on a sheet of paper. After your child reads the book, ask him or her to identify the five holidays discussed. Have your child write a few words that describe each holiday.

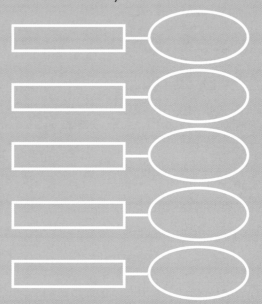

Vocabulary Lesson

Content words are words that are specific to a particular topic. All of the content words for this book can be found on page 32. Use some or all of these content words to complete one or more of the following activities:

- Ask your child to make a list of words that talk about a celebration.
- Have your child find words that characters use to describe something positive.
- Challenge your child to find two difficult words in this book. Have him or her use them in a sentence.
- Have your child find words that relate to each individual holiday.

Close Reading

Close reading helps children comprehend text. It includes reading a text, discussing it with others, and answering questions about it. Use these questions to discuss this book with your child:

- Why do you think the United States has holidays?
- Do you think some holidays are more important than others? Why or why not?
- Astro learned something new about each holiday discussed in this book. What did you learn?
- If you could create a new holiday, what would you celebrate and why?

Foundational Skills

A question word is a way to start a question. Have your child identify the words that start questions in the list below. Then help your child find question words in this book.

what	jumping	why	eat	how
hide	where	play	waving	sleep

Fluency

Fluency is the ability to read accurately with speed and expression. Help your child practice fluency by using one or more of the following activities:

- Reread this book to your child at least two times while he or she uses a finger to track each word as you read it.
- Read the first sentence aloud. Then have your child reread the sentence with you. Continue until you have finished this book.
- Ask your child to read aloud the words he or she knows on each page of this book. (Your child will learn additional words with subsequent readings.)
- Have your child practice reading this book several times to improve accuracy, rate, and expression.

WORD LIST

Astro the Alien uses the 118 words listed below. The words bolded below serve as an introduction to new vocabulary, while the unbolded words are more familiar or frequently used. You may wish to write the words on index cards and use them to help your child build automatic word recognition. Regular practice with these words will enhance your child's fluency in reading connected text.

a	dancing	happens	learn	October	special	**united**
about	day(s)	have	let's	of	speeches	US
all	different	hear	like	on	states	use(d)
also	do	holiday(s)	lot	other		very
Americans	home			our	Texas	**veterans**
and	ended		made		that	
are	**enslaved**	I	make	parade	the	
artists	Eva	important	many	people(s')	their	wars
asked	even	in	**military**	pod	them	watch
Astro		**indigenous**	Monday	presidents(')	there	we
	fireworks	is	more	**protected**	they	were
beautiful	food	it	music		things	what
beginnings	fought			said	think	when
Ben	fourth	July		school	this	where
by	**freedom**	June	native	second	time	worked
	from	**Juneteenth**	not	see	to	
can			November	should	today	you
	go(ing)	know	now	sing	told	your
celebrate(d)	good			**slavery**	**traditional**	
celebrates				some	travel	
celebration				space		
country('s)						

ABOUT THE AUTHOR

A. M. Krekelberg graduated from the University of Minnesota–Morris with an English degree. She has written dozens of books for young readers and edited hundreds more. When not writing or editing, she enjoys exploring Minnesota's North Shore with her husband and their hyper husky.

ABOUT THE ILLUSTRATOR

Carlos Aón was born in Buenos Aires, Argentina. He studied in a comic book art academy for four years. In 2000, he graduated as a graphic designer. Aón's work appears in dozens of graphic novels, story books, and educational projects in the United States, Argentina, Europe, and Asia.